Santa Mouse
Meets Marmaduke

MR. SQUIRREL

Santa Mouse Meets Marmaduke

By Michael Brown
Pictures by George DeSantis

Publishers · GROSSET & DUNLAP · New York
A FILMWAYS COMPANY

ISBN: 0-448-14749-1

Library of Congress Catalog Number: 74-92384

1980 Printing

Marmaduke Mouse was a mean little thing
Who often behaved like a rat,
He did things that weren't nice,
Like scaring young mice
By hollering, "Here comes a cat!"

His mother stayed busy—she ran Mouse Hotel
Up high in an attic, all hidden away
In a cupboard with doors,

MOUSE
HOTEL

WAX

Where she polished the floors
And she cooked

and she washed
and she cleaned
every day.

What Santa Claus had heard about him
He could not believe,
And so he said to Santa Mouse,
"Tomorrow's Christmas Eve.
Take off your suit and pack a bag,
Go down and ring the bell
And have a look at Marmaduke,
Who lives at Mouse Hotel."

So Santa Mouse packed up his things
(He packed a piece of cheese as well),
And off he went on Christmas Eve
To check in there at Mouse Hotel.

He left his luggage by the bed,
Washed up and then went down to dine,

And that's when Marmaduke crept up
And entered Number 29!

He tiptoed in—he looked around,
He opened the suitcase that he found,

And there inside he saw a suit,

Complete with hat

and beard

and boot.

"What fun!" he thought. "I'll get dressed up,
And I know what I'll do!"
But what he did when he put them on
Is sad to tell to you.

He looked into the kitchen,
And his mother wasn't there,

So he called his little sisters,
Who came scrambling down the stair.

When they saw him, what they did
Was burst into applause,
Because they thought on Christmas Eve
That he was Santa Claus.

Then Marmaduke pulled off the beard
And laughed and said, "You see,
There ISN'T any Santa Claus!
Ha, ha! It's only me!"

THEN . . .

A door flew open in that house,
And there stood angry Santa Mouse.
He said, "You KNOW that's wrong to do!
Just wait till I get through with you!"

He started after Marmaduke,
The little mice began to yell,

And pots

and pans

and apples

and

potatoes flew pell-mell!

The chase was on, with cups and saucers
Smashing, crashing from the shelf,
Till all at once, someone cried,

"STOP!"

And there stood Santa Claus himself.

"You mice have made a mess," he said,
And looked at them and shook his head.
"You've got to clean it up, you two,
And while you do, I'll speak to you.

"Now, Marmaduke, you told these mice
I wasn't real, which wasn't nice.

And Santa Mouse, you had a fit—
You lost your temper, you'll admit.

"And yet, you know, there's nothing wrong
With being angry, not as long

As you just SAY it and don't hit,
For no one wants that, not a bit."

And then he picked up Santa Mouse
And whispered something very low.
Quite suddenly they disappeared—
On Christmas Eve they work, you know.

As Marmaduke looked at his mother,
In his eye there came a tear.
"Sorry, Mom," he said. He knew
That he would get no gift this year.

But he was wrong, for in the morning,
Labelled with a big red pen,
A box stood there with his name on it,
Santa had come back again!

He opened it, and there appeared
(With cap and belt and boots and beard)
A suit that Santa Mouse had sewn
For Marmaduke to call his own.

The card inside said, "Let's be friends,"
And that is how this story ends,
As Marmaduke held in his paws
The proof there IS a Santa Claus.

Santa is a friend who's true,
And I believe in him.
                    Don't you?